These Dolls Don't Break

REGINA DRUMMOND

UNDERLINE
PUBLISHING

ISBN-13: 978-1-949868-31-9

Published by:
Underline Publishing LLC
www.underlinepublishing.com

For Nereide, a dear friend,
who helped me make a dream
of every author come true:
to take our culture further.

Index

The Porcelain Doll

I got home and opened the mailbox, mechanically, as I did every day. I was sure that most of the correspondence wouldn't be important. I had long realized that only fines and pizza advertisement use paper in these times of the internet. This time, however, there was something different: a package just over one inch high, no larger than my palm.

Still not that interested, but slightly curious, I didn't even try to guess its contents, instead I looked for a hint of the sender's name. And then, my eyes widened in surprise and excitement, my heart jumped out of my chest, and I started laughing as if the package I held in my hand was tickling me. For the first time, I was sure: she still remembered my existence! After years of absolute silence, she was now making contact with me!

Like before, she identified herself with the single C., as if everyone knew that she didn't need a full name to be complete, just the first initial and a small dot.

The funny thing was that it was enough. There was no address, only that one letter that said everything.

I stood looking at the package without the courage to open it. Despite my curiosity, the content interested me less than the feeling of being remembered by someone who had been a special person in my life. Knowing that she still remembered me left me so emotional that I soon went from the exaggerated joy of laughter to tears. The past jumped back and forth like a circus acrobat and, taking off his hat, in a traditional greeting, made sleeping images parade as if in a film, sweetly and in slow motion. And I could see her as I hadn't seen her in a long time!

Celia's life had always impressed me. From the beginning of our friendship, I had realized that her life had all the potential to work out, but she seemed dedicated with excessive commitment to doing everything wrong. I mean, maybe it wasn't quite that, but anyway, her actions had disastrous consequences and were always completely different from what I would have done if I were in her shoes. But I wasn't, and she had the right to do as she pleased with her life, especially since she accepted the risks and never complained.

Some people like to feel sorry for themselves and, when they make the worst decisions, it is as if they are looking for a reason to have something to complain. Most still insist on finding a "culprit" who exempts them from assuming their failures and understanding how much they are responsible. That wasn't the case with Celia. Her face showed an eternal smile, which could be more or less happy, but which remained a smile nevertheless. And from her lips, I never heard bitter or harsh words. She was a happy person from the inside out. However, I can say that she was a master in the art of deception and played her role perfectly, as if she lived on a stage, eternally playing the role of herself. She loved to play with fate, defying circumstances, and even death. It was no wonder that her secret dream was to be an actress.

Celia seemed to have only one goal in life, a goal which could be defined with one word: money. It wasn't as if she liked money in particular. She didn't care for it, but needed it for her greatest passion. A better description would be to say that she was a slave to money, subjecting herself to anything in order to have it. Yet, in some backward way, they had a "healthy" co-dependency, for money also was her slave. It was money that gave her all the kind of services and would facilitate what she really wanted: a better life.

But she wanted to get money the easiest way possible, since she didn't like hard or persistent work. In fact, what she really liked was wake up for lunch, spend time between the gym, shops and the beauty salon, taking a short pause to prepare herself to a night out, full of parties, only sleeping when the sun was rising. In the end, what she needed was a rich man who would take care of her and would give her the lifestyle she loved.

Did it have something to do with the cruel childhood that life had given her? Or with the even more complicated adolescence? Freud would say yes, Jung would say it could be. Myself? I don't know. But those who had all the details perhaps could understand her.

Little Celia was beautiful, with her confident strut and girlish look. She was so small and delicate that when friends referred to her, they didn't even bother to call her by name; it was enough for them to say "The Porcelain Doll" and everyone knew whom they were talking about.

Sweet and peaceful, she did not have the typical characteristics of similar people, such as insecurity, envy, jealousy, and competitiveness. It was as if she knew there was no woman more beautiful in the world than she was, exempting her from fighting or even thinking about her appearance.

To me, she was beautiful and delicate. She was not meant to be touched but only admired with respect and enthusiasm. Maybe that's why (although I'm not sure) she didn't need to sing to attract men like any mermaid—they only needed to see her. I'm ugly and boring, so, to me, Celia was a goddess, and I loved to go out with her on summer nights to admire the masculine landscape of the streets and bars. It never failed: we went in, she in the front, I behind, and we looked around as if we were waiting for someone (who had not yet "arrived") and sat down. In a few minutes, this or another "someone" would come and talk to us. Either dragged by the cascade of black hair that swayed with each movement, gushing down her back and almost splashing on the floor, or through her golden, slanting eyes that suggested more mysteries like those of an odalisque performing a belly dance. She received the candidates with a regal attitude, giving each one the classic fifteen minutes of attention, and then, making a charming pout, in which she expressed all her annoyance, looking around, already searching for the next guy.

It was the cue for my attack: if I stayed interested, I would immediately start a conversation appropriate to the guy's taste, and he ended up settling with me. I am ugly, yes, but friendly. I make the ugly-adorable-and-intriguing type, the intelligent and ironic lady of his destiny, irresistible characteristics for many men. That divided them into two distinct groups: those who let themselves be enchanted and who ran away, terrified. Well, the latter didn't matter, anyway.

I suspected that those men who stayed were more interested in the remnants of the possibility of having her, than in me, but that didn't matter. The guy would start by paying our bill on the spot, and then who knows where things would end up, in the range of infinite possible variations.

Celia always repeated a phrase, and she did it with such charm that it was as if she had just discovered one fatal truth:

"It's easy to find a boyfriend. What's hard is keeping one."

I always laughed. And although I never replied, I thought exactly the opposite! But I would let the subject die as we usually did with so many promising things, murdered for lack of adequate food.

The truth was, I just didn't want to share my ideas on the topic with her. I didn't want, not for anything in this world, to teach her my tricks, a mere illusion of any of the five senses, while she spoke directly to the primary masculine spirit. In fact, at that time, I didn't even know I had anything to teach.

Even so, I think you already understood the game: she attracted, and I captured.

Two experts.

A perfect match.

Probably because I was not a member of the Beauty Club, I thought I would have to make my way around the world through study, culture, the proper use of my intelligence. Although I bet all my chips on that idea, I believed that a beautiful woman could have everything she wanted. Beauty bought everything. There was nothing more vital than it as a bargaining chip—and

Celia was beautiful enough to have the man of her dreams kneeling at her feet, offering her the world, the moon, and the stars, among pink diamonds and cars of the year. It had always been like that since I had met her. And long before that day, I was able to sense it.

In the prehistory of her life, there were gaps and mysteries hidden at the deep of a sea that had no bottom, in one of those places so dark that the fish are blind and no one can reach it unless they use a diving suit and a good flashlight. So it was that I did. One day, I could discreetly glance between the tears that did not fall from her eyes and kept blinking, anxious. At the same time, she tried to keep the same smiling face, the misery hidden in the mud of a rough childhood. I think that was when the sequence of strange errors started, but I could not get anything out of that suffered sphinx, who had learned to hide the pain even from herself.

In the days of remote youth, when adulthood was far and not around the next corner, Little Celia chose a forty-year-old man as beautiful as a he was wealthy, with whom she married and lost two children. I suspect he had something to do with it, without proof. She clarified that she suffered more than she took advantage of what he offered her. She had enjoyed his wealth, but she didn't take it with her after the divorce. She did not become rich with the separation, so she had to continue seeking the security she longed for. But it was thanks to that first man that other, unsuitable men began to line up like in a domino game, one attracting the next, all different but incredibly similar.

I pressed the small package to my heart, still without the courage to open it. I saw, as clearly as if we were on a stage illuminated by the light of a powerful spotlight, the two of us sitting at a bar table: she, with her watery eyes attracting men, and I, laughing, choosing mine from hers. I thought her beautiful. I liked everything she did, laughed at everything she said, happy to be beside her, and to be able to share the joys of her beauty; me, for whom nature had been so thrifty.

When we first met, I was barely 20 years old and a happy newlywed who moved to a large and distant city, where I knew no one. She was the helpful, attentive, and available neighbor, always ready to help, a single woman, seeking to fill her own life. What she had the most was time, my most precious asset. Then she opened her apartment door and, in two steps, rang the bell to ask if I needed anything. At that moment, I knew I needed her.

"Hi, I'm Danilo. Can I sit?"

The scene changed so abruptly that I shuddered. The abrupt arrival of the first one interrupted my thoughts, which took a different turn within my memories. The smile Celia offered him was accompanied by that childish but bass voice, which was an integral part of her charm:

"Sure. Please."

She spoke like a girl who had been educated at a boarding school, the kind that nuns ran with an iron hand. Her gestures were smooth, befitting a lady. Her lack of culture she masked with a deep interest for her audience that seemed to be true. Sometimes she would nod as if she agreed with everything the other person said, with a discreet and elegant half-smile floating on her well-made mouth. Other times, she would shower the person with small questions that always stimulated him to speak more, sometimes between well-placed exclamations and involving looks.

When she got tired of the game or felt that the prey had fallen into the trap, the captive passed to me so I could do my part. If I were interested, it would last a little longer. If I preferred, one look was enough for her to understand that I had no interest in the guy. And then the next one came.

My thoughts repeated. I had seen this scene, but they were all so similar, that it was as if they were a single one, always repeated, repeated, and repeated again. A spoiled film. A nightmare. A recurring dream. I don't know. It was always the same. But how we had fun...! The goal was conquest, an end in itself.

We had long since realized that conquering had a special kind of pleasure, regardless of what happened next. Only that was exciting and was on it that the two Don Juan in skirts concentrated. The fun was playing with the prey as the cat plays with the mouse it has imprisoned: it squeezes it to feel the heart beat faster, it releases to pretend it doesn't want more, and then it grips more tightly; giving and taking away hope for freedom; enjoying the feeling of domination; and then taking possession like someone who owns a castle or a dream, which are the same in the end.

Oh! The smell of the past, the hidden memories, the mirages, the broken dreams; the packaged brought all of that even before I opened it! Specifically, I had my small realizations and a new possibility in the palm of my hand.

I thought it was better to get inside the apartment before opening the package. I had stayed too long by the mailbox, standing around like a fool, and I didn't want anyone to see my face when I discovered what was inside.

While I walked, I thought of how life separated people, so sweetly one could barely feel it. One goes this way; the other one goes another. Life took care of erasing the steps and only the memories remained, volatile as the essence of a perfume, attached to transparent glass as if they were an integral part of it. That was what life had done to us too: each took her direction, and I never heard from her again. Overnight, I became a famous writer, moved to another city. Familiar friends disappeared as the smoke from the thousands of cars circulated there. I was never informed about her again. Until the next fateful minute, in which I expected to find answers and news.

In the elevator, I kept thinking about the book I wrote, the one responsible for my meteoric success: it told the story of Celia's life. Very well romanticized, of course, totally disguised, but she would know who I was talking about if she ever read it. She wasn't much of a reader, but maybe. It was always possible for a copy to fall into her hands. No one would ever suspect my muse's real name, but for her, it would be as bright as the midday light. I had described her childhood in horror-movie-like details. I had invented an absurd adolescence for her, which hid the marks like the long-sleeved blouses she wore in the summer. I had spoken of her marriage as if I had lived it in her place. But there was no ending. The book ended without finishing the story, leaving a hundred doors open for life to choose and unleash the consequences, in the avalanche that characterized it - or not. I wanted to end it as I saw her life: open, available to the readers' imagination.

Critics loved the book and gave me all the awards of the year, but readers complained. They wanted more, a happy ending, or at least, an ending. Life is not like that; I answered them. Some say it doesn't end even with death. So, I left it as it was and did not get tired of giving these explanations in the thousands of interviews that I granted.

Thinking about these things, I lost the rush to open the package. I also wanted a happy ending for her, and I suspected that it would not reach me in that way, in a simple manila envelope of strange shape, without the return address. Slowly, I entered the apartment, looking at it and trying to guess the secret it was hiding and that was about to be revealed. I put it on the sideboard in the hallway and went to get a pair of scissors. I took another glance the postmark, trying to catch a glimpse of a city or place it was sent from, but it was blurry and didn't tell me anything. Only the label spoke to me, but as I didn't know Russian, it made no difference.

Finally, slowly, I took the courage to open it. It was an old cassette tape had a note with it: *I know you wrote about me. The end of the story will make another book. Kisses, C.*

She only signed C. Why add anything else?

Curiosity gnawed at me from the inside, and it hurt on the outside. I felt a chill in my bones and almost heard a suspenseful soundtrack. But I would still have to wait longer to know C.'s fate since I didn't have a recorder that played that type of cassette in a long time. And where to find one, at that late hour, when all the stores had already closed their doors?

I called a few friends heartily, cursing her out loud while typing on my cell phone, but gently, saying things like: "Girl, you're out of touch! Nobody else uses a cassette tape like that!" I wondered if she was in some lost village in Siberia, close to the end of the world since she had gone to Europe with that husband she called a Doctor. Anyway, that had been my last piece of information. A long time had passed since then and she might've the time to go around the Earth three times with one of her temporary millionaires. There was no reliable information there, but that made the package even more intriguing.

I insisted until I managed to locate a friend who owned an old recorder, the kind I needed. He lived far away and didn't want me going there so late, so he tried to convince me to leave it until the next morning, but I couldn't wait any longer! I went back to the garage, started the car, and turned the radio on to listen to international romantic songs that made me remember her and our nights in trendy bars.

She was so beautiful! But so many years had passed; had she changed at all? Memory does not film, it photographs. But I could still see her walking towards me, one step at a time, light and harmonious as a cat, fluid and fatal; a smile always floating on her lips. Then she would throw back her hair and look at me with her yellow eyes, saying some charming nonsense.

I missed her a lot, I had a great urge to talk to her and tell her about my life the way I could never talk to anyone else. I wanted to ask her, and listen to her, to admire her while speaking in her different and unique voice.

I drove monotonously down the long avenue of limited speed, with my thoughts so distant, in another time, in another space, almost in a previous life.

My idyllic wedding didn't last long, and we both soon set out on our way to find other partners — and had a lot of fun searching, of course, since the search itself was known to be the best piece of the cake. We were so young. Everything was beginning. We thought we had our whole lives ahead of us, and an occasional failure didn't faze either her or me.

People in my family considered me crazy, and they said no man would stand me the way I behaved, but I knew I only had a real interest in life, and its name was "book."

Since I was a child, I wanted to be a writer. I read day and night, despite my mother's insistence. She ended up forbidding me to read (an order I never obeyed, anyone is quite capable of imagining that!). When I got tired of reading, I wrote. My first novel was ready when I was 12, to the horror of the family, who thought that all writers were crazy. Perhaps that was how my reputation as a crazy person came to be.

But there was nothing a good marriage didn't fix, and an exciting candidate soon presented himself. And he was ready to get rid of my addiction! Yes, I did get married; maybe to test things out, but it was inevitable: I soon realized that I would have to get rid of my husband to cultivate my addiction better. And that's what I did.

The world became, between a written book and several readings, Celia and me. She didn't like to read, but she was my connection with the so-called real world, the home of those whose lives I didn't have the power to manipulate. When she left with that foreigner, I was alone with books. The only way to rehabilitate me was to publish one that was so successful that even my family was proud of me.

It was great. My eccentricities became funny and... Sorry, that didn't matter. Now that Celia was back, I must confess that I hoped, in the most secret corner of my heart, that she finished her tape informing her flight schedule and asking me to pick her up at the airport.

Thankfully, books are not usually jealous because they would have to be without while I took care of her. I didn't understand why she chose this weirdest form of communication, but I would find out in a bit.

Between one thought and another, between memories and comments to myself, I went and returned without haste to the other side of the city. The tape player on the passenger seat remained quiet and dumb. I didn't want to hear a story, which I hoped to be fantastic, in the middle of the traffic, although now more peaceful, but always an uncomfortable place. I wanted to enjoy every minute with her, at home, silent and attentive as if going to a movie theater. I was sure the story would be worth it.

Did she still send money to her mother and siblings, through the bank, as she did before? She knew they never called her, but she didn't care. She continued doing what she called "the duty of the good daughter," doing it every month, without thinking about it. In truth, she only had a real interest in life, and its name was "her beauty."

The Porcelain Doll was the vainest girl the world had ever produced. I didn't believe she differed much from any famous model. I know that she wasn't able to make millions walking on the catwalk or being featured on the cover of magazines like the characters that populate the imagination of ordinary mortals. Despite this, she lived to take care of herself, and her worries lived in her silky hair, in her little princess body, in her round nails painted in light pink. Outside of that was the world that only really existed when a man with an expensive wallet approached.

I came home, put on my pajamas, smiling at my thoughts, and settled on the couch, legs curled and head resting on folded arms. Then, slowly, I reached out my right hand and pressed play.

The emotion was so great that I held my breath.

A few vast seconds took their time before bringing her voice to me. The world stopped to hear her. I could see that she still had the same serious but deliciously childish tone suited for a porcelain doll.

It started with an apology for never responding to

my letters, remembering that she didn't like to write, which made me laugh. The truth was she couldn't write and was ashamed of making thousands of mistakes. She also apologized for not calling. She explained that it was costly, and the Doctor was stingy with the phone bills. I didn't laugh for fear of missing a word, but it could only be some new joke. Before I left the euphoria of imagining this scene, she started talking about the subject in question:

"You will not believe the direction my life took. My husband is a doctor, you must remember, and he has a fascinating job. I started to help him to fill the time. The day can be so long, in the towns where we sometimes need to live… I did simple, but essential services—you know me!"

She laughed, and my laugh echoed hers, even thousands of miles away. It didn't matter what she meant by that; it was still the same laugh, which was filled with her distinct sense of humor. I felt that she was so the same that I couldn't know if her mood preceded the laughter or if it was the other way around. I had a condescending thought, as if I was her mother, always willing to forgive her beloved daughter's mistakes with a naughty smile and that nod of the head that says: "Children are like that, they do such crazy things!"

The Porcelain Doll's voice continued:

"I… He… Do you remember what his job was

like, a little mysterious? Later on, it became even stranger, but now it doesn't matter anymore, the world has already learned about the new techniques that he and his colleagues developed so that I can tell you everything. When the mystery was unveiled, the dead dazzled the living! You must have seen it in the papers."

She laughed again, but now I didn't like it. No, I hadn't seen it and was already getting impatient. She couldn't get out of the prologue, and I almost went ahead, but it was so good to hear her voice that I stopped myself. It was as if she was beside me; looking and speaking only to me.

So I endured all the little turns, the comings and goings, the repetitions, the catchphrases, and the evasions, until she started to talk about what I wanted to hear. But I think it is better you hear it yourself.

"Marcela, I know that my vanity is a disease. Still, I cannot live without feeling beautiful before the mirror, beautiful before the world, without dazzling anyone who looks at me. I have to be attractive to men, envied by women, and adored by children. I need to feel the admiration in people's eyes. Otherwise, I will die. You know this. And I haven't changed.

I always wondered what it would be like when I got older. But this is something that usually only happens to other women. So I sent the thought away as if it was contagious disease, and ran to the mirror to see if my eyes were still bright as the sun, if my skin was smooth, and if, if, if…

Despite repeating that beauty is nothing more than an accident of nature, the Doctor also loves it in all the forms it takes, including the ones it uses so he can pretend to be humble. He works as if he has a mission to keep beauty in one of these forms, even when it disguises itself and is sad and horrible. As beauty is excellence for him, he only knows one way of doing things: beautiful and perfect. That makes us close to each other; it offers us a common goal.

I always thought he was a doctor like any other. Perhaps, in the beginning, he was. He chose to be a coroner because he liked death. He explained to me one day. The autopsy allowed him to search for the actual cause of a person's passing in the story their body told— he was something between a psychologist and a detective, with a mind-boggling passion for anatomy. He is a writer who does not write, but unveils the secrets of the soul and weaves long and intricate novels with skins, bones, and fibers. That overwhelming interest attracted the search for something that had significant meaning and contributed to the world. And he went further, much further. On one occasion, we visited a German university, and he met another anatomist even more insane than him. Together, they defied death to preserve life, as they think that no matter what type of life it is, it will always be bigger than the opponent. For them, certain types of life can camouflage the seed of immortality within them."

She sighed and paused. I smelled death in the air, but it was pure anxiety. That delay in the narration, the suspense to tell the secret, was what was killing me.

A strange song played in the distance as if it were part of the story. It must be a movie, I thought, on the neighbor's television. She spoke again, and I continued to listen eagerly.

"Then something happened that made me want to live forever. I will be the Doctor's first guinea pig, but I'm sure it will work. And if it doesn't, it will be worth the try."

I had to stop the tape for a moment to absorb the revelation. How was that possible? I wondered. I'm going crazy with them!

She continued as if she had not realized the overwhelming force of what she was telling me, as naturally as if had nothing to do with her:

"Two years ago, a colleague of the Doctor, a highly regarded doctor in Germany, diagnosed a rare type of cancer on my face, which has a difficult and painful treatment. He said that my face would change little by little, I would become someone else, not pretty, of course, since the disease would deform my appearance. To put it simply: he had no way of eliminating the diseased cells, and they would grow until it would take over everything. In his language, "not pretty" was a euphemism for "monster." Imagine if you will: first, the skin would become scaly and rough. Then, lumps would grow in all directions, including branching and reaching other areas.

Of course, I didn't want to believe it—let alone accept it! Nothing in my body showed any sign of the disease! A few weeks ago, however, when my skin started to look like an alligator's, I thought he might be right and decided to end it all. I spent long hours choosing how I wanted to die because it had to be in a way that preserved my beauty. I could never accept that the people who saw me beautiful all my life, would remember me all busted, like a character from a book that you once described to me! Something like that? Never! That story shocked me so much that I remember it even today!

It was so that wouldn't happen to me that I wanted to leave this world—and, since I had a choice, to do it delicately. So hanging, drowning, jumping off the twenty-first floor, taking poison, causing a car accident, throwing myself under the train, killing myself, becoming a woman-pump, and other such deaths were out of the question. I had to cut my wrists, but that didn't seem particularly pleasant.

Suddenly, I understood that my body had a much more glorious destiny and, full of happiness, I told the Doctor about my idea. He didn't immediately agree, but I suspect he just wanted to test me.

For me, it was immortality. To him, it was a way to eternalize my beauty. To keep it intact, and even to have me, finally, just for him. But it was much more! Because he also knew that we would open new paths for science, enhancing the art to which he had dedicated so many years of his life.

I can explain. Until that moment, the Doctor had only worked with corpses, meat destined for putrefaction, which he bought from human butcher shops: remains of injured strangers, who would be buried as destitute; very poor dead people, whose family was happy with the possibility of receiving some money in exchange for a dead man who the worms would eat for free; bodies of people who believed in him and the work he was doing and, therefore, had been destined and donated to him in life. Regardless of origin, what came to him were the remains of what had once been a human person. Now, the possibility of working with a living being was knocking on his door. And soon, he started to plan how he would do it."

At that point, I had to stop listening. I pressed the pause button and took a deep breath, trying to hold back the vomit that came up hard, biting my dry mouth. On my way to the bathroom, my head threatened to come out of my neck, the floor sank, and the walls spun…

It was a horrible story, but, despite the anguish that squeezed my heart, I freed the thoughts that flowed like water from the glaciers towards the river, cold and heavy like the blocks of ice they dragged. They wanted to take the form of threats and chants, but I pulled them from me because I intended to judge neither small Celia nor the Doctor—at least, not before hearing the end of the story. I had to keep an open mind, free from prejudice, to understand the absurd logic that was trying to emerge from madness.

I made a tea from boldo leaves, although I knew my stomach was in perfect order. I wanted to feel better to endure what was coming—I knew what was coming might be much worse!

"Crazy, Celia!" I thought, going back to the couch and pressing play.

"I bet you're horrified! But don't worry: the crazy guy who invented this has already plastinated his best friend!"

I didn't even have time to absorb this information, since she asked without the slightest pause:

"Have you heard of plastination?"

I didn't even answer. Celia continued:

"I suspect you haven't, so that I will give you a summary. I promise to be quick, in case the answer is yes. You know, our body is made up mostly of water. In plastination, organic substances are replaced by plastic material—silicone, epoxy resin, and polyester. That allows these wetted parts to acquire plasticity, that is, they remain malleable, odorless, and dry. The body is as if it were made of plastic, hence the name, plastination. Perhaps you have seen some exposure, several have already been done, and I know that you are a well-informed woman. But I will continue to tell you because it is my personal view of my husband's work.

When whole, the plastinated body can be admired in all the divine perfection of someone who was created in the image and likeness of God. Still, it can also be broken apart, piece by piece. The identification of the parts is very interesting: here is the heart, there the lungs, there the liver, can you see the tongue inside the open mouth, with all the teeth? That mouth has lips, and at the bottom of it are the tonsils. Anyway, what's inside is truly there. It is a real person who is there. There is no possibility of error!"

She laughs. Her laugh, even mocking, is crystal clear, happy. And she continues:

"For comparison, you can see a healthy lung next to a smoker's lung, for example—and it is said that many people stopped smoking when they see this! Or a healthy organ alongside one with cancer. Anyway, it's fascinating, I guarantee you!

But there is more: you can appreciate the bones, or the muscles, or even open a window in a woman's belly and see the baby curled up inside, perfect as the baby was about to be born. And the "sliced" bodies? I can't explain it; you have to see it for yourself!

The muscles seem to be the most exciting. The

Doctor immortalized athletes in their prime moment of splendor, with the body in motion: the volleyball player when jumping to cut the ball, or the soccer player with all the muscles taut in front the goal, or the athlete winning the race, the swimmer arriving, the ballerina on tiptoe. Ah, he does the same thing with the animals' bodies, so that the horse and rider, for example, are exposed. It is gorgeous! The exhibitions attract thousands of people.

The first objective of plastination was the study of anatomy. Still, it ended up being transformed into art: "anatomical art," which has been going around the world to be admired by laypeople, since plastinated bodies acquire properties that facilitate handling and cutting, becoming also moldable and, above all, transportable.

But that is all now in the past. I am the future. The present is the search for a plastinated, but alive being, with all its functions preserved. So our goal is for me to see, smell, hear, feel. If so, I can have sensations of touch and taste. I will be alive, although I cannot participate in the world. I will not be a zombie, much less a vampire, because, as all my organs will be asleep, I will dispense with food as to maintain life.

I think you understand: I will be as dead—or asleep if you prefer—but conscious. One day, when a doctor finds a cure for my illness, the process will have to be reversed, and I will be ready to start living again."

I couldn't listen anymore and took another break from the tape. The idea was monstrous, but I must admit it made sense. Furthermore, it was not the first time that people had dreamed of conserving their bodies or immortality. I sketched a wry smile, wishing that Sleeping Beauty would come back to life the way she always had been, beautiful and kind. Just then, I remembered other attempts, in which the dead returned aggressive and bloodthirsty. It had to be different from her; otherwise, it wouldn't be worth it. I wished that her beautiful golden eyes did not see the world as if it were the first time, but as if she was coming from a trip, or just woke up with the sun.

I made more tea, now with mint, thinking that if some people were frozen a few years ago, why couldn't others be plastinated?

I didn't expect this to happen to "her"... But I soon realized that what I felt was jealousy and tried to control myself. It was in vain. A dull rage began to bite my soul and sour my words.

What an empty creature! She didn't care about the people who liked her! As if she didn't know she had friends or family! No human being mattered more than her useless cardboard beauty! What good is beauty for? I wondered. For nothing! I replied. Nobody eats or drinks beauty. It doesn't even serve to ensure happiness! You can't even touch it— you would feel the object where beauty is, not beauty itself!

Just admiring isn't enough compared to the trouble it causes! You know what? Beauty be damned! And it should take with it all the vain people on the planet!

At that moment, I felt that I hated not only beauty but also hated this futile porcelain doll that I loved so much!

It is well said that love and hate are the two sides of the same coin, that the opposite of love is indifference. Because I reached out to start the tape again as if I hadn't interrupted the story to fight with her, and just as casually as if I had turned it off for some other reason. I was curious about the ending. I shouldn't have expected much from her, the champion of open-ended stories, without finishing or finishing off. However, I still thought she wouldn't do that to me and wouldn't leave the end of the story to my imagination!

In the first few words, I was sure that she had heard my screams, had read my thoughts, or penetrated my heart, because she continued, candidly, as soon as I played the tape again:

"You must hate me now, finding me futile and empty, concerned only with something useless, destined to disappear. But that's not true, so I don't care. When you consider my words with love and compassion, you will understand."

She paused for so long, and I feared it was over. But I was wrong. She soon continued:

"In closing, I want to warn you that the process will begin tomorrow, May 2. I mean, when you get this tape, I'll be already over there. Please, dear Marcela, rejoice. I was hoping you could think of me as someone who has achieved nirvana. I am so happy, so peaceful. I am at peace as I have never been before. That's all I expect from you, my best friend, the only one I've ever had. And I want you to know that there was never anyone in this world for whom I felt a love so complete— because it was so honest—than for you. Believe me, we will be together forever.

In about six months, I'll be ready, and I would like to receive your visit. Look into my eyes and be sure that my soul has found eternity."

She sang a lullaby and said nothing more. The tape player stopped on its own, but I still stood there for a long time, thinking, until I fell asleep without knowing how. Maybe I dreamed about her; I don't know. I only remember a pair of golden eyes shining more than the morning sun.

Alternative Life

Tatiana liked to stroll through the cemetery, and not just the one near the subway station that served her neighborhood. She loved any cemetery and made a point of meeting everyone who crossed her path. When she traveled, any time she reached a new city, the first thing she did was take a walk in the cemetery.

She walked along the paths slowly, carefully and deep in thought.

Sometimes the paths were large and decorated with trees and sumptuous tombs on the sides. Others had narrow streets with uneven pavement. From time to time, they looked like cities, while others were nothing more than empty streets, with a hint of abandonment that pleased the young woman.

No matter what style, there was always the coolness and calm adorned by cypress trees and the hundreds of dried, peeled, dying flowers. The wind used to blow, running like a wild horse, or sweetly, caressing the dead leaves, which scratched the ground with its roughness. The wind intended to be pleasant in the summer. In the winter, it was always cold.

Tatiana knew that the wind held all the secrets but only revealed them to the chosen ones. She always liked it, even when it was a breeze because the wind was the biggest gossip of all time! In the absence of new secrets, the wind continued to reveal old ones, which made it fun and, at the same time, ridiculous in its eagerness to spread the secrets that were not its own while pretending to protect them.

Above all, the cemetery was where no one bothered her—especially in the middle of the night, which was her favorite time.

"Yes," thought Tatiana, while walking. "For this and other reasons, this is the most pleasant place in the world."

This was nothing too strange, due her condition, but even so, her love for cemeteries was exaggerated!

Every day, before dawn, when she came back from work, she would walk around the tombstones slowly, paying attention to all the movements and traveling within herself while reading the names and dates that she knew by heart.

Jamir Augusto dos Santos – 1912 – 1981
Anna Barthmann – 1894 – 1957
Stefanie Rosas de Almeida – 1948 – 1949
And so on.
Tatiana laughed.

The dead were of no interest at all, but it was funny to wonder what kind of life these people had in this land of misery. Well, wondering was not quite the right word. If she wanted to know, she only needed to caress the photograph or the name carved in the stone, and then she would see it all with the eyes of her fingertips.

That Stefanie there, for example, was a pink baby who had come for a short mission: to unburden the heart of a cruel woman. Or to turn it to stone for good. Stefanie had accomplished her purpose very well: disgusted with the death of her daughter, the mother had dropped her mask and shown the person she was: an evil person, exceptionally selfish, who didn't care about anything besides herself and her goals.

However, most people were unimportant people, those so-called reasonable creatures, manufactured in series, all the same, a speck here, another there, not to say that the creator had no imagination, rarely something grand and worthy—inferior beings. But sometimes, ah, one only needed to look to find the exceptions that justified the rule.

Tatiana worked as a graphic designer, from 11 pm to 5 am, in an advertising agency, after classes in college. That was her official job, the one that paid her bills, but she did freelance projects, and that extra money allowed her to travel and buy clothes from famous brands without worrying about bills.

She was proud of the normal life she led. She was working as if she needed it to live, attending university as if there was no other way to acquire knowledge, traveling by car and plane on holidays and weekends, as if there were no different kinds of transportation, relating to people as if she was one of them, deceiving them with such skill that no one even dreamed that she might not be what she seemed.

She even had a boyfriend now. A strange human, but still not strange enough to be admitted as an aspirant in the community to which the young woman belonged. It didn't matter. For now, it was fine. Tatiana had learned to avoid dramatic situations—hunger and fury, for example, were undoubtedly the worst. She managed to be an almost normal girlfriend, the type who worried over her lover and taking care of him as if he hadn't left childhood yet. But she couldn't display certain paranoid attitudes, so ordinary in relationships— like jealousy and hysteria, for example. But people could live with these little flaws.

Women could disguise themselves very well with makeup—there is no paleness that a good blush could not color! And the rest was just details. Incidentally, tiny and banal.

"How cold your hands are!" her friends would say at the beginning.

"Women and children have cold extremities," she taught them.

If they didn't know already, they had just learned. Even these and other comments about her body temperature no longer made sense. Nobody had noticed that she avoided touching people and she would make clear that she didn't like to be touched. Easy to manage.

The dark glasses solved any problem that her photophobia could pose. The "allergy" to the sun was understandable. Wearing black clothes was a symbol of elegance, so Tatiana could be mistaken for any normal woman, walking the streets. Now, finally, she could have the normal life she had hoped for. And it wasn't even that difficult.

Of course, not everything was flames, as the demon would say. And she, too, had already faced horrible situations. The worst of all, no doubt, was when someone cut themselves and the blood welled up, firm and hot, brighter than gold, redder than the forbidden fruit. If she were a human, she would say her mouth was salivating, but since she was from another race, she had to clench her teeth, look the other way and fight the mind-boggling desire.

After many centuries of escapes, persecutions, and deaths, Tatiana had reached a stage that, if not ideal, could be said to satisfy her fully. She didn't use to miss those old days, but she had a few tantrums from time to time.

Times of war had been her favorite. She could make a man disappear and the maximum punishment was for him to be dishonored as a deserter. She could make women disappear and nothing would happen. Even children disappearing had no consequences, as no one would notice they were gone. There were hundreds of people lying around in the streets ready to be snatched. A paradise. It should've been like that forever. But humans are now registered, and easier to track using statistics.

For special cases, she went to the most remote places on the planet, where life is insignificant, to indulge herself. She did not always find good blood, the full-bodied type, but it was enough for her to cure her anemia. Bad blood is better than none.

But everything gets boring.

One day Tatiana got tired of that relentless search for food. She felt like an animal, living only for survival. And the situation became horrible. Terrible. Unsustainable. Something unworthy of her immortal and superior condition. For even humans lived for something other than the simple act of feeding. Luxury, for example, was an essential food of human arrogance. No, she couldn't go on like this. She had to look for another life. She decided to change.

That became possible when the eternal young woman made an exciting discovery: she could eat almost fresh blood to maintain her strength. It wasn't exactly "drinking." There was no way to compare that already clotted, hardened thing with real blood. Of course, it was not the same. But it did deceive her nature.

Her passion for cemeteries grew to the maximum, and she was always looking for information about recent burials, so that, in the dead of night, she could lick the open veins of the dead.

The operation required delicacy: with the tip of her sharp nail, she opened the artery horizontally and did precisely as a cat would do with its milk bowl.

Has anyone tried giving powdered milk to a cat?

Tatiana even suspected that she might've liked it, but the truth was that when people were hungry, they could accept any food. So clotted blood might not be the same, but it worked.

That was what she was looking for in her delightful and lonely nights at the cemetery. Then, (almost) sated and satisfied, she strolled through the streets and alleys as if she had discovered a new way to help her digestion.

One day, Tatiana took too long on the walk between the graves, while waiting for a funeral to end. When she returned, the ceremony was over, people had left, and even the gravediggers had finished their work.

The silence was absolute. Not even the wind had come to tell its stories. With her keen ears, she realized that something strange was happening: sharp blows were coming from inside the earth.

Experienced, she thought without emotion: "That one was buried alive. Let's see how she is."

As Tatiana pushed the flowers away and lifted the stone covering the tombstone, she thought of the deceased, a girl still young, dark-haired and beautiful, whom she had seen lying in the dark coffin. She had been in an accident that shattered her chest, but her face looked like it was carved out of marble, beautiful and perfect, with regular features and a mark that split her chin in two with lots of charm.

Her screams were now understandable:

"Help! Somebody get me out of here!"

With her vampiric strength, Tatiana performed the entire operation with ease as if ripping a dress, releasing the girl almost instantly.

Frightened, she was even more beautiful. Her full dark eyes had been opened wide by panic.

"What happened? What am I doing here?" And placing her hand on her chest, she sighed. "It hurts so much." When she saw that a trickle of blood dripped slowly, staining the whiteness of her blouse, she exclaimed, even more stunned: "What happened to me? This must be a nightmare!"

Tatiana was unable to control herself. Her canines jumped as fast as the pounce she gave, but she still managed to hold on and looked the girl in the eye, mesmerizing her.

They looked at each other for a moment. One, cold and calculating. The other, frightened and helpless. Without knowing how, Tatiana saw herself leaning over that open and inviting chest, exclaiming:

"This is a dream! This is a dream!"

In her longing, she did not mind that warm, sweet blood covered her face and hair. On the contrary, she rubbed her bloody hands and licked them, longing, with the despair and greed that only obtaining something long dreamed of provided.

The girl melted in Tatiana's arms without making a single sound. Her body was getting heavier and heavier. Tatiana dropped it in slow motion on the grass, thinking that she hadn't felt that happy in years.

Loud and robust, Tatiana shouted her joy, raising her arms, victorious. Unable to contain herself, she punched the air and jumped the crazy choreography of the winners. Then she started to laugh and couldn't stop shaking her body, laughing with the elegance of the gargoyles. The sensation was pure delight!

Later, when she calmed down, she threw the emptied body back into the grave, with determination closed it with the heavy stone, and smiled a Mona Lisa smile, narrowing her eyes with long, delicate lashes.

For humans, nothing had changed. But for her, something fantastic had happened: her essence demanded a return to her origins. Tatiana looked around. Always smiling, she added, gloriously: "I'm done eating grass!"

She spread her wings and took flight, startling the birds and animals of the night that landed on the branches of the cypress trees.

A Story of Women

Gina saw the creature and sensed that it had been watching her for some time. Paralyzed, both faced each other—for minutes? Seconds?—but neither moved. The other one for some unknown reason, perhaps even inexplicable. However, Gina's motive was as clear and transparent as a glass of fresh water: she just couldn't stop. Dread had frozen her limbs, leaving her without action, without movement, and without will. Despite this, her brain remained the same—agile, canny, and efficient—and she thought about how stupid she had been when she agreed to go to that place, knowing what could happen. Now she was desperately trying to command her body:

"Get out of here! Move! You still have a chance to escape!" she thought to herself.

The conductors carried the messages, but panic had closed all connections, causing the words to be lost in the hiatus of madness that separated the threatened young woman from the macabre figure. Cold, Gina kept looking at those dead, static eyes that conveyed no emotion—except the one she knew so well, but maybe that was just a morbid fantasy. A chill ran through her body from top to bottom, bristling pores wherever it reached.

Although she could never control the creature in such a simple way, the young woman wanted to command it with dry orders like: "Get out! Move! Go way!" Gina knew everything she needed to say, she could even think of the right words, but they wouldn't come out of her closed throat and died like waves on the beach, gently bubbling and turning the air.

Terrified to the fullest, Gina made movements with her tongue stuck inside her mouth, wanting to scream, call someone, ask for help, but her vocal cords had hardened forever and not a moan left her dry, pale lips. Nor did her eyes move, wide-eyed, glued to the thing, fixed on the one who had come to get her, indeed even more furious after several failed attempts.

Precisely because her body was immobilized, Gina had the feeling that her brain was accelerating, clear and sharp, traveling in time and space with even greater precision and more speed, shuffling memories. However, her brain was focused on the creature in front of her, as her memories focused on other encounters they had had. Everything converged on the creature and led to the phases of her previous relationship with that "thing," who took immense pleasure in tormenting her.

For how long had that hideous creature been chasing her? Gina had lost track of time and was unable to answer any question, not even a simple one, in thought, from her to herself.

What the damn creature wanted was another mystery, which Gina no longer remembered the answer for it. All she knew was that she could do nothing against that disgusting being, which had the power to paralyze her. It was certain that the other one was the strongest. And it wouldn't be long before that was painfully clear.

In desperation, she dared to dream that someone would come to her rescue. Still, it was as if she had moved to another dimension, from where she could see humans—their movements, their conversation, the expression on their faces, their gestures—but they couldn't see her, not in the way she saw herself: alive and healthy, although maddened with dread. That was because they were on the other side, separated by glass or a transparent film that made contact impossible. Only she was on that side: she and the damn thing.

It could also be the other way around, she thought, feeling herself freezing even more. Perhaps she had become invisible to the world and visible only to the creature, but that didn't matter because it didn't change anything. She would be just as unhappy, in a position of inferiority, at the creature's mercy, available, delivered and dominated by that round and dark look, which threw her into an endless and never-ending hole. The creature had evil eyes, which kept her a prisoner of her spell. Hypnotizing eyes. Snake eyes.

Snake. The word brought to Gina's mind a long fat snake looking at the little mouse huddled in the corner of the wall. One waved its forked tongue. The other waited for death. Hypnotizing eyes. Vampire's eyes. Vampire. The word brought the image and raised the alarm. Gina's heart beat like a drum; even faster, the blood ran through her arteries and went around her body.

It didn't make sense! If the creature was interested in her blood, it still hadn't shown that preference. For the time being, it seemed to enjoy the panic in her eyes, the numbness in her body, the despair in her heart—the victim's doom! Torturing her was all the monster wanted. It seemed that driving her to despair was enough. But until when?

That made Gina's memory go back to a time in the past: another time they had met and she miraculously escaped.

It was night. The moon was shining in the sky. She was in a hot, inexpensive room of a "just one-night" hotel. She read a book, totally disconnected from the world; sweetly enveloped by the magic of words, she traveled with the characters, when, suddenly, without the slightest warning, the demonic envoy entered the open balcony and looked at the young woman with that look of something recently dead (although all Gina wanted was for it to have been dead for a long time).

The book fell on the bed without a sound. The night closed its curtains, and time withdrew, stopping the clock. Gina missed the action. Her whole body stiffened up, waiting for the next act that would not come: motionless, both measured with their eyes.

While she was terrified, Gina lost control over her body. It had been that way since she was a child. Gina was an active and independent woman who earned her livelihood and paid for luxuries, a strong woman who had never feared anything real she could face head on. But she became a statue when it came to facing that creature who now met her with an alien and amorphous look as if it had just arrived from another planet and tried to recognize in this land the places it had traveled to one day, the other monsters it had lived with, and the situations it had experienced. As if that had any importance! As if that were possible! As if at that moment, something else could exist besides fear!

Sometimes Gina didn't understand why the goddamn thing wasn't going to end her right away. Or why Gina didn't try to end the creature. Gina could also kill it and end the matter. Why didn't she do it? Gina knew the answer: because she couldn't. She just couldn't.

But what could be worse than the dread she felt? Was the disgust worse than that horrible feeling of helplessness, fragility, of being at the mercy of the whims of someone who dominated her?

The other, however, seemed to appreciate this absolute dominance so much, this terror it inspired, that did not put an end to the unsustainable situation. And why would she do that? It should be a delicious moment for her.

What would the creature feel? There was no way to know. It was undoubtedly made of another matter. The best it could do was rotating the antennae, without taking its eyes off the poor, terrified girl's face. It didn't smile, but there was no doubt that if it could do it, it would be a false smile, one made without open lips; or cruel, twisting and tightening its mouth in an evil grin. Perhaps the creature smiled on one side of its face as if the other was paralyzed. But it had never greeted Gina, not even when it retired, proud, regal, and owner of the world, in a pose that showed its dominance and magnanimous.

It was so arrogant, that thing. It was alive but often seemed dead in its exasperating immobility. Its head was small concerning its body, how could it be possible to fit so much evil in such a tiny brain? Yes, its malignancy lived there. It didn't have a heart. But moved, walked, attacked and frightened, causing even horror and disgust—and it was perfectly happy doing that, the sadist. Gina knew that she was not the only one to feel terrified by the creature's approach, even when it pretended that its intentions were the best possible or when it was itself fleeing from a predator.

Yes, the repugnant sometimes just crossed the path of mortals, distracted and preoccupied with its affairs (or problems, who knows!), without caring about them. It was just passing through. It went from place to place where it could happen to have someone in the middle of the road like a stone, but it was just that, a speck, nothing, less than a flea, more insignificant than the most trivial of beings. It passed by without looking and disappeared without a trace. Who saw, saw, who hasn't seen, never more.

The disgusting creature knew how to express itself, it was even quite eloquent, but speaking, it did not. It passed seedlings from side to side. It appeared and disappeared without moving its lips. It kept looking and waiting, always with its mouth closed. It attacked without a word, safe, precise. It might as well talk, but well, it couldn't do that. Or it had never done it, which could not be said to be the same thing.

It was ugly and disgusting and vulgar, but it was not afraid of Gina; Gina was the one scare of it. And that was what bothered the poor girl the most!

Gina had never been afraid of anything in her life; much less fearful of life. Her mother had raised her, a poor and honorable woman, who had worked hard to be someone but had died before seeing what her daughter had achieved. But from somewhere, or wherever she was, she would be applauding the young girl, standing in the front row, and her eyes would be filled with tears when she saw the leafy tree that that little seed she had planted had become.

Gina's grandmother, a little lady who everyone saw as sweet and kind, was always around, more interfering than helping, it was true, but the neighbors didn't imagine any of that, that was the family's secret. She never looked at others in the face. Shyness? That was what they said.

At that point in her reflections, Gina imitated her grandmother and looked sideways at that creature that was able to control her like a puppet. It was still the same way; it hadn't moved a millimeter. But life was always moving forward; her grandmother died without discovering the evil and falsehood that lived in its soul, the monstrous creature disguised as an angel. When it spread its wings, it brought darkness into the world. Wouldn't that creature be the reincarnation of your late grandmother?

Gina shook her head to get rid of such thoughts. The involuntary movement severed the connection and had the power to return her to the present reality. Then she saw a young girl who was staring at her, her eyes full of curiosity. She was about seven years old and was sitting across from her at the restaurant table. Her curly hair was straight and tied in two pigtails on top of her head, one on the left, one on the right. Her eyes, black as the darkest night, looked as sweet as two blackberries.

"Are you afraid of it?" asked the little girl, pointing.

Gina shook her head, confirming.

So the little girl said, very seriously, "I'll take care of it, Mom."

And getting up quickly, she used her delicate little foot, wearing a cute little shoe, to stomp on the monstrous cockroach. At the same time that it was crushed to death in a crash of thunder, it released white, shiny goo, the only reminder of its passage through the world, which remained there, standing out against the darkened brown of the floor wood, before other feet, inadvertently, eliminate it from the face of the earth.

A Brown Cat Like Any Other

She was a delicate and straightforward cat, like all cats are. She liked to stay on top of the wall, where she posed with elegance, her tail always fixed at her side, bathing in the sun. Or she dozed off, curled up on herself, looking absent, but linked to the slightest movement. Sometimes, she did her lengthy grooming, licking her hair in every corner and nook of her body. From time to time, she would walk around and around as if waiting for someone, then jump down and disappear among the plants.

I tried to approach her without success. She allowed a distance of one meter between us, looked at me, meowed, moved away halfway to the side, and ran away—typical of skittish cats.

There were many apartments in the various buildings that formed the complex where I lived, so it was impossible to know who owned the cat. Unless I started to ask, which might seem strange and even arouse suspicion. Discreetly, I had already questioned the doorman and the gardener, but they didn't know how to answer, so I soon gave up continuing the investigations.

I fantasized about her as if she were a person. I couldn't think of anything else. It was like I was in love. What kind of life would she have? Who lived with her? Was she loved and cared for? Did she have a basket to sleep in, a plate for her food, toy mice to play with?

I was sure she didn't have any of that. The cat was thin and scared; the short coat was brown and lackluster, with scars here and there from old fights cropping up and vivid eyes hiding a greenish sadness among the brown streaks.

"She is going to be mine!" I thought.

I looked in my storage for the little bowl and the small plate I had used previously in similar situations. At the supermarket, I bought cat food, the best and most expensive they had on the shelf. I arranged food and water in the corner of the fence, and observed what was going to happen, sitting on the garden bench, hidden behind the sunglasses and pretending to read a book.

On the first day, she came closer and closer, looking around, suspicious as only a cat knew how to be. She ate quickly and jumped to the side and over the fence.

The next day, she came towards the food again but did not look around as she approached. When she got very close, yes, she looked for some sign of danger and, not finding it, ate quietly. Then she left at a brisk pace.

On the third day, she came and ate, knowing it was for her; when she was satisfied, she left quietly.

And so, that was how things went. I arrived before and put food and water in the respective containers; then, I walked away and watched while she walked with all elegance, ate without haste, left without looking back.

Gradually, I was showing myself to her. I let her see when I put her food on the plate, so she would know who was taking care of her, caring for her, wasting time with her.

She looked at me with her huge green eyes, but waited for me to get away before approaching.

She never seemed to be starving, but she always ate well. Either way, cats are in no hurry, a quality we shared. They choose, not just accept, what is given. They never eat anything without smelling it here and there, waiting a minute and tasting it again. Even when they hunt, they like to play with their prey: they also release it to see it run away then run after it to catch it again. Diabolical animals!

Sometimes, I thought I already deserved permission to cuddle, but she disagreed. As I approached, she ran. I was frustrated, but I didn't change my attitude or retire my intentions. I just decided to wait for a better time.

We continued our game for a few more days, and she was always skittish and reclusive. Gradually, however, she calmed down, and got used to being near me, maybe thankful for all that work I did for her.

"You're a very curious girl," I said, sometimes to her, other times to myself.

I'm glad I learned to appreciate difficult things. Deep down, I thought that the harder it was to have, the stronger the taste of victory, so I kind of licked my lips in anticipation for I would get in a little while! I just needed to be patient.

Nothing to do, but follow her day after day. Finally my day came, and she, for the first time, with her eyes full of fear, allowed me to touch her.

I can say it was my moment of glory: it was the reward for all my efforts.

Seized with an intense, almost physical emotion: my breath held, my hand stretched out to her, my fingertips touching her soft fur, I bitterly smiled as if to apologize for feeling my heart pounding, my mouth dry, my eyes half-closed in feline fashion. I bent down but slowly, so as not to startle her. I stretched the body, and still, without breathing, I passed the hand flat on her back, to which she seemed to correspond, adjusting the body for my touch.

I stroked her until, perhaps because I squeezed a little harder, she jumped away.

I was happy, but I still wanted more. I wanted her to come spontaneously to my lap, eat in my hand, and trust me completely and totally.

I knew it was just a matter of time, and time was something I had to spare.

I continued with the treatment, and she responded, continuing to allow me to caress her.

One day, I managed to pick her up and bring her to my chest. She reacted, hardening her body, and trying to escape, but I scratched behind her ear, and she softened, softened, until, finally, she relaxed and let herself be caressed.

It was like a password. I felt accepted. From there, I could touch her, carry her, caress her. More and more, she seemed to enjoy being on my lap.

One day, she purred softly. *Prrrr.*

How exciting!

It looked like she had a motor in her chest. And I understood that my moment had come.

I placed her gently on the floor and walked away, slowly, anticipating that magical moment.

One second, one step, another second, one more step, and it was as if my legs were the hands of the clock, always moving forward and toward the goal.

I felt my mouth full of water as if I was dreaming of a tasty treat, but it was only the anticipation for the joy that awaited me. The memory of what would happen made my heart race so fast that my temples ached.

The next day, when she came to eat, there was no food in the bowl. She arrived, searched, stopped, sniffed again, and stood looking around, her eyes full of questions.

I was waiting for her, sitting on the bench, a book beside me and with a lap full of cat food, but she couldn't see it. I showed a small piece on my fingertips, and she took two steps, confident, to smell it. Loving what she felt, she took it with her teeth with that typical feline delicacy and sat on her hind legs to taste it. I gave her a sign, and she understood, climbing onto my lap unceremoniously and preparing to get fed up with her favorite food spread there.

The longed-for moment had arrived!

"Ah, you silly thing! You thought could escape me, did you?" I joked, grabbing her by the neck, which made any cat harmless as a dead worm.

She tried to run away, scratch, and bite me, but it was impossible. She was immobilized. She could barely kick and meow, totally without action. In a minute, I stuffed her in the burlap bag I had always prepared for these cases. Then I got up and calmly walked away.

I gave her the same fate that I had given to all the other cats I conquered and convinced to trust me.

The Bird

The rain was falling outside, sad and small. The street was empty. The late afternoon washed away Sunday, leaving boredom to spread across the sidewalk.

Beatriz was concerned. She wanted Monday to come soon, for her to get rid of it, to make that decision that was so heavy, threatening to crush her. She looked out the window, anxious as if an answer could fly by and help her to give the final word on the matter.

She strode through the small apartment once, twice, three times, returning to her observation post as if she were a watchman. She looked outside for the millionth time. The trees were gone. The streets were a long, bright corridor. Behind the glass, she saw her mother in the hospital's ICU.

Her eyes closed on her colorless face already denounced her dead, but she was still breathing, helped by the machines. She didn't move a muscle. Maybe just the diaphragm, so faintly couldn't even tell. She lived because the monitor informed so.

What would she think, watching the hours run away without haste? Would she remember the times of her youth, the good times she had in her life, or as a spiteful person who had always shown herself, demanded everyone what she thought they owed her, and only thought about the things that had displeased her?

Now, Beatriz was sure she would never know. The mother's condition was irreversible. She would never be what she once was. The brain had been damaged, so there was no chance that she would recover. They would never speak again. They would never look at each other in the eye. Never again would she feel camaraderie, sympathy. They would never fight again. Never.

"My mother is an undead," thought Beatriz. "But not even the fresh blood that drips into your veins can bring it back to life..."

She smiled a smile that was nothing but a bitter grimace. Not talking, not seeing, not listening, maybe not even feeling, did that deserve the name "life"? But how to make sure that she did not see, hear, and feel nothing?

Perhaps she felt all the emotions possible for human beings in perfect self-control. If she saw when Beatriz arrived, if she found out that her daughter was going to visit her before going to the office, every day, religiously, at 6 am like someone going to mass, maybe she would feel love, affection, tenderness, she would perhaps felt loved, cared for, protected. If she were able to think about her situation, maybe she would feel anger, revolt, or even a deep acceptance would envelop her.

Perhaps.

If she were in a hurry to heal, she would undoubtedly feel anxiety, anguish, and despair. If she were in a hurry to die, she would undoubtedly feel sadness, fragility, and helplessness. But in any case, the physical pain that the medications tried to soothe but were unable to extinguish completely, and the feelings of weakness in the face of the situation should be like Tantalus' torment.

And Beatriz was thinking about Tantalus, the rich and powerful king of Phrygia, who claimed to be the son of Zeus with Princess Plota. He loved Dione, the goddess of the nymphs, and he had three children with her, Pelops being the youngest. As he was very vain, Tantalus began revealing secrets from the gods to mortals. Then, to test whether they knew everything, he committed a horrible crime: he killed his son Pelops and served his meat as an exquisite delicacy at a dinner with the gods! Of course, they realized, raised Pelops, and punished Tantalus, condemning him to suffer from thirst whnile close to the water and from hunger near where there were beautiful trees laden with fruit—only he couldn't reach either one or the other. To make Tantalu's suffering worse, they kept a rock suspended in the air, just above his head, which made him feel the dreadful fear of death. The expression "torture of Tantalus" refers to the suffering of those who desire something close, however, unattainable. It was precisely how Beatriz felt at that moment, still fantasizing that her mother felt the same.

Her life was not unlike that of Tantalus: every morning, the sun brought hope that things would work out. The day made her feel better, despite everything, but already the night came. Despair was installed, to be driven out by the morning sun that brought hope, hope that never materialized, but crystallized in the night full of despair, that the morning sun amazed, to put in its place the tip of hope that led her to live another day, even knowing that today would be the same as yesterday and tomorrow would be no different than today.

The sadness of the feeling of helplessness, she knew it well and there was nothing to reduce it! Where would the mother find room for joy, in that limited and tasteless life?

Hope is the stone that moves the world, that drives us forward. Perhaps she still had that absurd hope, which made her believe that tomorrow was going to be another day. Probably not even her vegetative state could destroy hope.

Every day, Beatriz took her mother's hand and said: "You can't imagine how much I like you!" But she didn't know if she could hear, feel, perceive, or even intuit her words. Her mother didn't return her affection and, from her wax face, no movement or expression indicated that she had understood the words or sensed their meaning.

Beatriz turned her thoughts back to the good times they had lived together. Her mother was a strong woman and thought it was her duty to control her feelings. She wanted to appear cold, but she hadn't been cold, instead she had been a good mother. She had taken care of her daughter with affection and dedication.

When Beatriz was a child, the two of them played together, amid cheerful laughter, and her mother read stories to her that spoke of fairies, witches, giants, and gnomes of a magical world. Along with their father, they traveled for camping, especially on summer weekends.

She delivered her school reports to her mother, which not always had good grades, hoping that she would calm her father down, although he was not even exceptionally severe.

Time passed. Beatriz grew up, graduated, got married, became a brilliant professional, had children, separated. Her mother, in some way, was always by her side. And Beatriz knew that she could count on her for everything she needed.

Now, after months of torture that remained stable, stabilized, always the same, without any worsening, but also without any improvement, the doctor had asked her for a decision.

Beatriz stood at the window of her apartment as she had been standing at the hospital window, after that last conversation, looking out with the empty eyes of someone who sees nothing, when a dull thud interrupted her thoughts.

She blinked to return to the present but saw nothing. The mark on the window glass, however, confirmed that it had not been an illusion.

Beatriz turned, took two steps, and opened the balcony door. A bird lay on the ground. Beatriz bent down and picked it up, settling it in the shell of her hand to better observe it.

It was beautiful and delicate. It had mixed brown plumage in varying shades and a small yellow tuft. Its two little legs were curled up, and its body was thrown aside. Its open eyes were glossy, but it was still alive. Its rounded chest rose and fell weakly, a little accelerated like someone who had been startled or surprised.

Beatriz didn't know what to do, and she looked at it for a moment. The bird seemed to return the questioning look.

Beatriz took it inside the apartment, striding towards the kitchen, where she dipped the tip of her index finger in the tap water of the sink and offered a drop to the bird, which it was unable to accept.

Beatriz opened its beak, and a fraction of a drop of

water managed to pass. The bird's long tongue came and went from its beak, restless, in the various attempts to drink, while the bird gave her grateful looks, but at the same time, implored something indefinable.

Beatriz shook her head and muttered: "I'm seeing things…"

But the look was there: a thread that connected them. The look of someone who is not sure if they had died. A look full of pain. A look begging to be freed from suffering.

Beatriz felt like crazy. Complete. Now it was possible to understand the language of birds! No. Much worse. She had never been able to know what birds wanted when they chirped or even sang with grace. But she knew what that still, empty, and expressionless look begged for. She didn't want to believe it.

She looked again at the tiny bird lying on her left hand. A wing was broken. The neck, half on its side, wasn't able to hold the head. That sweet little head that shouldn't have weighed more than a few measly grams now weighted as much as an elephant.

Weaker and weaker and without strength, the bird gave her those hard looks, which seemed to beg for something that she well knew what it was, but did not want to accept.

"Please," the bird's eyes seemed to say. "Please."

Suddenly, Beatriz realized why that look disturbed her so much: it was the same one that her mother gave her each morning when she laid half-dead in the hospital bed.

She couldn't take it anymore.

Closing the shell of his hands, she brought the bird closer to the body and cradled it like a tiny baby. She delicately passed her finger on its yellow tuft, trying to caress it without touching the broken wing, not to bring it more suffering. She placed another drop of water on the tip of the beak, which only opened when she forced it. Beatriz admired the fragile tongue, so weak that couldn't move anymore.

She shook her head, full of pain. She understood what she had to do. She understood that not prolonging the suffering of any living being was part of the obligations of a just person and she no longer had to think about the decisions that awaited her. The speed of thought surprised her, but it wouldn't stop her from doing what had to be done.

She looked again at those pleading eyes and, in a sudden gesture, twisted the bird's neck at once.

About the Author

Regina Drummond was born in Minas Gerais and today lives somewhere between Munich, Germany, and São Paulo, in Brazil. She wrote more than 130 books mainly for children and young people, translated many others, but what she likes most is storytelling. Her work has been translated into other languages and has received awards and highlights, including the "Jabuti Award," from the Brazilian Book Chamber, as an editor and a nomination for the same award as an author; she also got "Highly Recommendable" and "Basic Collection" stamps from the National Children's and Youth Book Foundation, which represents IBBY, in Brazil.

Official website:
www.reginadrummond.com